In Over Her

Head

By Porsha Deun

Books by Porsha Deun

I'm on my Snoop Dogg with this dedication.
I dedicate this book to me, myself, and I!
This past year plus has been a struggle and full of a
lot of change.
I persevered.

In Over Her

Head

Chapter 1

Kareema sat in the lobby of the one of many law firms she called the day before. Both she and her new business were in deep trouble before the company got off the ground. She needed help. Major help.

Jones & Associates was the only firm within a one-hundred-mile radius willing to see her after the initial free phone consultation. Because of that, Kareema felt they were her only hope. When they instructed her to turn her phone off before arriving at the office, she ignored the uneasy feeling in her stomach.

The receptionist, with skin the color of unfiltered honey, sat at the desk in the small lobby. It seemed to Kareema the receptionist got paid to do a lot of nothing, as the woman was putting a clear coat on her long, white painted nails while laughing at something she was watching on her computer.

Kareema shook her head at the lack of professionalism, but then thought about her precarious predicament. She had no place to judge.

"Where do I know you from?" the receptionist asked while pointing the polish brush at Kareema.

"I can't say we've met before," Kareema answered. The last thing the twenty-four years-old wanted was to be recognized by anyone.

The receptionist turned her nose up. "Snoody much." The woman narrowed her round eyes and popped her tongue. "I know I know you from somewhere."

Just then, Ms. Unprofessional's desk phone rang. She picked up the receiver. "Yes. Uh-hu. Okay." She hung up the phone. "Mr. Jones will see you now."

Kareema stood up and waited for the receptionist. After a few moments, the woman looked up from her show. "What?"

"Which way?"

"Down the only hallway and to the only door that has Octavius Jones written on it."

"Oh, my… wow." Kareema marched off down the hallway until coming to the door she needed. With her hand on the doorknob, she closed her eyes as if to say a prayer when she heard the receptionist gasp.

"That's the chick on social media that's been making everybody sick!"

Kareema quickly pushed through the door and closed it behind her. Still with her eyes closed, she leaned against the door, willing the receptionist to stay at her desk.

"Ummm, Mrs. Monroe?" a deep voice asked.

Kareema, startled, opened her eyes, and found a handsome man in a crisp black dress shirt and gold tie sitting at the desk. The man's walnut complexion was blemish free and his deep brown eyes seemed to sparkle. His well-trimmed thick beard and mustache framed his face handsome.

"Are…are you Octavius, I mean, Attorney Jones?"

He stood, revealing his tall athletic frame and black dress slacks. Kareema was not expecting for him to be so damn fine. The handsome attorney walked around his desk and put his hand out for a handshake. "Octavious, please. Have a seat."

She walked to the cracked faux leather chair in front of the desk as he returned to his seat. "You have quite a case, Mrs. Monroe."

"Kareema. Just Kareema. I'm not married."

"That is good to know, Kareema," he said seductively before licking his full lips. "To make sure I understand everything, go over your situation again for me."

"Well, I had an idea for a condiment sauce. Something people would love as much as they do ranch dressing, but is not ranch dressing, if that makes sense."

"Not at all."

Kareema sighed. "It will once I explain. So, I took some ranch, added a citrus pop to it—"

"Pop? Like pop pop… soda pop?"

"Yeah, there's more, though." Kareema ignored Octavius as he placed a hand over his mouth. "Citrus pop, water, milk, a bunch of garlic powder and oil, red pepper, lemon pepper, black pepper, salt, cornstarch to thicken it up, and a bit of ACV."

"ACV?"

"Apple cider vinegar, you know, for a little tang. Oh, and red and blue food coloring?"

"Why add food coloring?"

"I wanted the sauce to be my favorite color, purple."

"So, you made this concoction—"

"The Every-zing Sauce."

He nodded slowly. "The Every-zing Sauce." He paused for a moment before continuing. "You made it, bottled it, and sold it to people online."

"Yes. I swear people were loving it, and now there are haters threatening lawsuits claiming I made them sick, but they can't prove it was my sauce."

"What preservatives did you put in your sauce?"

"About that part. I didn't know I had to do that."

Octavius stared at her in disbelief. "So, you didn't send your ingredient list off to the FDA for approval?"

"I didn't know they had anything to do with things that weren't medicine. I mean, do all the other dressings and mayos go to the FDA beforehand?"

"Yes! Any packaged food item sold on shelves at mass goes through the FDA approval processes. This is precisely why!"

"Oh."

Octavius took a deep breath. "You shipped them how?"

"The post office."

"No, no. What type of packaging?"

"Bottles from the dollar store and plastic envelopes."

"Insulated plastic envelopes with an ice pack to keep it chilled?"

Kareema shook her head.

"Did any of your customers complain about the bottles expanding or exploding?"

"Yeah, but that was because of the post office being rough with packages."

"No, again. That's because you used ingredients that should've been refrigerated or at least cooled with an ice pack in properly insulated packaging, and they developed bacteria because they weren't kept at a safe temperature."

It was clear to Octavius that Kareema didn't mean to hurt anyone. She was trying to get her bag. Unfortunately, she didn't think her plan through. Now she was in over her head with potential lawsuits from customers, and fines and jail time once the health department caught up with her. He had a way to get her out of the mess she was in, but only if she was willing to give him something.

In Over Her Head

Chapter 2

"Are you saying my sauce… I got people sick?"

"You definitely got people sick, and they have every right to be angry and sue your company. You won't lose everything because they can only sue the LLC, not you directly. Do you have your LLC paperwork with you like we talked about yesterday?"

"I wasn't sure of what paperwork you were talking about. I made the online store and put LLC in the name. Doesn't the business automatically become an LLC once it opens up for sales?"

"Are you telling me you never file articles of organization with the state?"

Kareema didn't respond. His words were foreign to her.

"Do you even have a DBA?"

"Great," Kareema sighed. "The only lawyer who would see me is making me feel stupid."

"I apologize. You may not have the business smarts you need and desire, but you are an ambitious and exquisite woman."

Kareema couldn't even take in his compliment. "That will not save my business."

"I'll be honest with you. You never had a business. What you had was a misguided experiment that you tried to pass off as a business. You missed so many steps that this… thing you started never had a chance. Shut everything down, issue a statement and send emails to those foolish enough to buy your experiment to instruct them to throw it away immediately."

"But I just got a facility at the new building over on Dale Road. I quit my job to get this started."

"Dale Road? Please tell me you are not talking about the storage facility they just built over on Dale Road?"

"My contract is for $140 per month!"

"That is not suitable for preparing food! Kareema, I know you meant well, but this isn't it. You are the latest internet villain and people are ready to dox you. I've seen the videos."

"If you already knew you couldn't help me, why bother having me come in at all?"

"Like I said, you are an exquisite woman. I wanted to see if the beauty I saw online was the same in person. Are you dating anyone?"

"No, and I don't want a slimy attorney to be my man."

"You may find my ways slimy, but you have little of a choice. As you said yourself, I'm the only one willing to see you, and we both know you can't afford me."

"So, you want to fuck me for payment?"

"I want you for payment."

"How is that different from what I said?"

"Did you tell anyone you were coming here?"

She shook her head.

"Good. So, what that means is, from this moment on, I am your man. I am going to do all I can to protect you, but you must do *exactly* what I tell you to do."

"What is that?"

"Do you agree?"

Kareema was confused and angry. She planned to use her sex appeal to get him to provide his services for free, or at least a major discount, by giving him some head a few times. Even buss it wide open one time since he was so fine, but Octavius turned things around on her. If she didn't agree, she'd have no choice but to deal with the fallout of her failure on her own.

She couldn't do that.

"I agree."

Octavius laid out a plan for Kareema and her child, a three-year-old boy named Koraan, to disappear. She was to pick her son up from the sitter's, go home, and call her mother to inform her they were going to lie low for a bit because people were after her.

It wasn't a completely false story, so it would work.

Kareema followed those instructions exactly. She was grateful she got her mother's voicemail when she called. She left her apartment of almost six years and got into a black SUV with tinted windows, taking just her diaper bag and purse.

Her driver, a bald, dark-skinned black man with dark sunglasses and a hard expression, took off into traffic.

"How do you know Octavius?" she asked him.

Radio silence.

"Does he do this often? Uproot women's lives to take them for himself?"

Again, the man said nothing.

Except for the sound of Koraan's tablet, the ride out of the city was quiet, much to Kareema's ire. The SUV drove into a posh suburb that Kareema had window shopped in since she was a child. She imagined one day she would live in one of the mansions that sat on massive amounts of land.

"No way," she said under her breath. She wondered how a lawyer, a Black one at that, with an office in the heart of the hood business, could afford to do anything more than drive through this area as she had done.

The SUV turned up a driveway that wound through tall trees. Kareema noticed a brick wall just past the trees that seemed to go on forever. When she looked directly ahead, there was a large iron gate.

"Phantom approaching," the man said. That was when Kareema saw the walkie talkie. The gate opened as they approached. There were men in black suits on the other side of the gate. A couple of them had machine guns strapped to them, while others had no guns that were visible, but Kareema was sure they were armed as well.

Kareema didn't know what she had gotten herself and her son into.

Chapter 8

Octavius' house was the biggest she had ever seen and sat at the top of a hill, elevated above the rest of the grounds. There was no way to count the number of red and black bricks that glistened in the sunlight. Black shutters and tall white columns complimented the bricks, as well as the perfectly manicured green lawn and bushes. This amount of exuberance was unreal to Kareema.

She could've easily celebrated this quick come up for her and young Koraan, but this terrified her just as much as losing everything because of lawsuits.

The SUV drove halfway around a small round garden of sculpted bushes before coming to a stop in front of steps that lead to the front door of the mansion. Another black suited guard opened the door and Kareema got herself and her son out. Kareema decided then to refer to the guards as *suits*. The woman standing next to him greeted her.

"Welcome, Ms. Kareema. I am Mrs. Knowles, and I will tend to you and your son's needs. Let me show you to his room." She looked at the suit next to her and he took Kareema's bags. Mrs. Knowles headed up the stairs and Kareema followed. Two more suits opened the tall French-doors with an iron ivy design.

"Okay, what does this man do for a living?" Kareem asked no one in particular after they stepped into the foyer. She spun in a slow circle, looking up at the ceiling that had to be at least twenty feet high and had a large crystal chandelier. The chandelier cast rainbows in every direction in the foyer and the grand staircase within it.

The suits remained silent as they stood around in the foyer, but Mrs. Knowles responded. "That is something you will have to ask Sir Octavius."

"Sir?"

"I've worked for this family for many years, Ms. Kareema. Your son's room?" Mrs. Knowles stood with her hand out toward the stairs.

Kareema nodded. They all continued up the grand staircase and down a couple of long hallways until they reached a large room with pale blue walls, a queen-size bed, and toys galore. The two-bedroom apartment she just abandoned could fit inside the room. The suit put the bags on the bed and left without saying a word.

"I told him yes only two hours ago, if that."

"Sir Octavius has had all the staff preparing for your arrival since yesterday," Mrs. Knowles answered. "There are clothes and shoes for your son in the closet and personal care items in the en-suite."

Koraan pulled away from his mother and started going from toy to toy, excited to see so many toys in one room.

Mrs. Knowles's words shocked Kareema. She realized now that her new beau had been planning this since they talked on the phone the previous day. "How long have you worked for this family?"

"I started as an evening nanny thirty-one years ago, just before Sir Octavius was born. I was only sixteen then. Six months into the job, his father, Sir

Darius, offered me a full-time, twenty-four seven, nanny position that required me to live here with my schooling being finished with a tutor. As time went on, I came to run the entire house."

"How did your parents feel about you leaving school to live with another family and take care of their child?"

"Sir Darius went to my parents first. They… needed help and were already in debt to him."

"Are you saying your family sold you to Octavius' father?"

"They did what they had to do. I hold no ill will towards any of them. My parents did the best they could, given their predicament. Honestly, my life has been better for it. As a child, I went to bed hungry many times. I haven't experienced that since coming here."

"Did you… do you have siblings?"

"Yes. A sister that I still see from time to time. She used to work here too, but it was not a good fit for her. I had a brother." After a few moments of silence, Mrs. Knowles went on. "My life has been better here. I even found my husband here. He runs the kitchen. I'm sure you will meet him later."

There were more questions Kareema wanted to ask, but they were not questions for Mrs. Knowles.

"So, what do you think?" Mrs. Knowles asked. "Is there anything you would like changed about your son's room?"

Kareema stuck her head into the ensuite and walk-in closet. "This is… perfect. Too much, but perfect. Where is my room?"

Mrs. Knowles gave her a soft smile. "With Sir Octavius. He wants to show that to you himself when he returns for the day."

Kareem huffed. "Of course." She forgot for a moment that she wasn't just a guest. She was *Sir Octavius'* girlfriend.

"Will you be needing anything? I can have the kitchen send up some snacks and refreshments. Dinner will be served once Sir Octavius comes home."

"Yes, that will be fine."

Mrs. Knowles left the room, closing the door behind her. Kareema sat on the bed, trying to wrap her mind around how her life had drastically changed in a matter of hours. If it was for the better or worse, she didn't know. The one thing she was sure of was that Octavius was not as simple of a man as she assumed him to be.

Chapter 4

Hours later, there was a knock on Koraan's bedroom door.

"Yeah," Kareema called out.

Octavius walked in. From her position on the bed, Kareema admired how the large door opening didn't dwarf him. Octavius walked in without a word, took Kareema by the hand, pulled her up and into his arms. "I've been waiting all day to do this." He planted a firm kiss on her lips that took her by surprise. Octavius coaxed Kareema's mouth open and plunged his tongue in.

His kiss was overwhelming for Kareema. She tried to pull back a bit to change the pace of the kiss, but Octavius only pulled her closer to him and he grabbed a handful of her ass. Kareema put more effort into pushing him off, and this time he let her go.

"Hi!" she said sarcastically.

"Hi." Octavius gave her a wide smile.

"In front of my son, really?"

"You're right. I should have introduced myself to him first." He walked over to where the child was playing in the middle of the floor and kneeled to his level. "Hey, little man. Your name is Koraan, right?"

The boy nodded.

"Well, I'm your daddy now."

"Octavius!"

He stood, picking Koraan up with him, and gave Kareema a look that told her not to challenge him on the matter. "I'm not his daddy? We're not a family?"

Kareema nodded.

"Tell him."

She walked to where they were. "Koraan," she started with a shaky voice. "This... this is your daddy."

"Daddy?" Koraan asked.

"Yes, your daddy!" she said with faux enthusiasm. "This is your daddy." She knew her son wouldn't know any better, as he had never met his real father. Hell, Kareema never knew how to find him.

Koraan was the result of a drunken one-night stand in a club parking lot. She and her son's sperm-donor met on the dance floor. He kept up with all her winding and grinding, which impressed her and made her think he would be good in bed. The way they continued to dance, they might as well had been having sex, so they did. Outside, against the stucco wall of the club. Other than swear words as moans, they didn't exchange words past him asking her if she wanted to fuck and her agreeing with a nod.

Kareema told all of this to Octavius in his office earlier that day.

"That's right, little man. I'm your daddy. You see all the toys in this room? Your daddy got those for you. You see your big boy bed? Your daddy got that for you, too."

Fear set into Kareema. A part of her didn't want to believe that such a nice and generous man would be dangerous, but the way he had deebo'd his way into her and her son's life was unsettling. She fought to hold back the tears that were welling up in her eyes.

Chapter 5

"Sir, Miss," a female voice said from behind us.

I turned and saw Mrs. Knowles standing by the door.

"Dinner is ready."

"Thank you, Mrs. Knowles," Octavius said. He took Kareema's hand and while still holding *their* son, he took them to the formal dining room on the first floor.

The dining table was much too large for the three of them, Kareema thought. She knew no one else was joining them, as there were only three place settings. Octavius pulled out a chair for Kareema, then walked to the chair opposite her and sat Koraan down in it before sitting himself at the head of the table.

They were served street corn, strips of grilled chicken breasts, greens with smoked turkey, and grilled pineapple, which Koraan loved.

"What is it you really do?" Kareema asked. The question had been burning her mind for hours. A part of her feared the answer.

"I am a fixer of sorts."

"What does that mean?"

"When someone is in trouble or is being done wrong by someone, I help them out as best as I can."

"What trouble was Mrs. Knowles's family that required her to leave her family to come to yours?

"That was before I took over the business and changed it to something more... positive. My father was a drug lord. A very successful one. Everything that moved through the city came from his organization. Anyone that tried to move in was shut down immediately. One good thing my father did was build the trust of the community. Yeah, he was pushing the things that were killing the hood, but he dealt with those that were doing stupid crimes and shit."

Octavius took a bite of chicken. He continued after swallowing it. "Mrs. Knowles's parents were junkies. They owed their drug dealer, who was my father's employee. The dealer felt sorry for teenage Mrs. Knowles and her siblings. I mean, they were just kids with parents whose habit was more important to them than they were. Knowing my mother was pregnant and held mistrust for the woman originally hired to be my nanny, the dealer came to my father. He suggested hiring Mrs. Knowles so she could provide something for herself and her younger brother and sister."

"Why didn't your mother trust the original nanny?"

"Because she was my father's mistress. The woman wanted my mother's position…and for me to not exist. In fact, she tried to suffocate me when I was a few months old. My mother and Mrs. Knowles caught her. My father was livid."

"What happened to her?"

With emotionless eyes, Octavius stared at Kareema before answering. "She went away. That didn't stop him from taking other mistresses, though. He made it clear to them where they stood."

A pit settled in Kareema's stomach, and she put her fork down.

"I'm not my father. You don't have to worry about me sleeping with another, but I am quite possessive of all that's mine." There was a heavy silence in the dining room.

"So, you're a drug dealer," Kareema asked, to break the tension in the room.

"No. I do not run the business my father did. With his death, there was an opportunity to start clean and to clean up the mess his operation had made of the neighborhoods. Most of the drugs I turned in directly to the police. The rest was used to set up the dealers under my father from the largest to the smallest. Because of that, I have a lot of influence with the police departments, D.A.'s offices, city councils, mayors and managers in every city, township, and village in the tri-county."

"You still haven't said what it is you do now."

"I'm a fixer. The checks and balances of the neighborhoods and their governing parties. If a landlord slacks on their responsibilities or raises rent by a ridiculous amount, we encourage them to sign their properties over to me with a phone call to the city office. A police officer steps out of line, they then lose their job and home. Someone makes a foolish business decision… I get them out of it and if I can, save the business for a return."

Kareema went to say something, but Octavius put his hand up to stop her.

"Not your business. There's no saving that. I own many of the strip malls in the county and have investments in many businesses, local and otherwise. I also own several houses and apartment buildings, including the one you were living in."

"You own my apartment building?"

Octavius nodded. "That is why I told you not to worry about it or your credit. The office knows to leave the apartment just as you left it for three months before getting rid of it and to not file an eviction with the court."

"What is it you expect me to do here?"

"Be happy and grateful."

"I mean with my time."

"You aren't talking about another business, are you?"

Kareema rolled her eyes at him. This wasn't the first time she felt like he was mocking her entrepreneurial spirit.

"Let's take the time to find something you are truly passionate about. Once we do, we can build a team around you to help you be successful."

Kareema nodded, but she wasn't sure if she trusted his word. Then she thought of something. "Why are you posing as an attorney?"

"I never said I was an attorney. You, and many people, assume that the first time they call or come into the office because of the name, Jones and Associates. That is just the name of the fixing side of my business, where people can have their grievances heard."

"What is the rest of the plan?"

"No one can serve you if they don't know where you are. No social media. In fact, I had you give me all your credentials so I could delete all of them. You are not to leave the property at all for a year."

"A year!"

"People must forget about you. Because you pissed a lot of them off, you need to become a phantom for a little while."

"What about my mom?"

"You already told her you were lying low."

"Not for a year! You expect me to go a year without seeing my mom? For Koraan to go a year without seeing his nana?"

Octavius looked over at Koraan for a few seconds. The boy was oblivious to the very adult conversation happening in front of him, as well as how drastically his life had changed. "Would you feel better if she moved here?"

"You would put my mother up in a room here?"

"Yes, well, not in the main house. There are a few guest houses on the property. I will have the staff set one of them up for her, so you can always have access to her."

"Thank you."

"I can be a reasonable man, Kareema."

Once again, Kareema wasn't sure what to make of her new beau.

He wiped his mouth with a napkin and tossed it onto his plate. "Let's go. I want to show you and our son some of the property."

In Over Her Head

Chapter 6

Octavius showed them the fruit, and vegetable gardens, as well as the flower garden his mother started. He bragged about the property's many amenities, like a mini-golf course, basketball court, shooting range, pool, and guest houses. After riding in a golf, the new couple put Koraan to bed. Octavius took Kareema to the French doors at the end of the same hallway her son's bedroom was located.

"Wow," she said as she walked in after Octavius opened the doors. People usually made the bed the focal point of a bedroom with a bunch of plush pillows and patterned or colored comforters. In Octavius' room, the bed was the focal point because it was massive and sat on a platform in the center of the oversized room.

"The bed is custom made. In fact, everything in here is."

"It would have to be. The posts on a normal four-post bed are not that tall or wide. And the mattress is…"

"Larger than a California king mattress."

"Why do you have a bed that big?"

"Because I can. And it's our bed now."

Kareema looked around the room that was even larger than Koraan's new room. A sitting area on either side of the room, one with a coffee and tea bar and the other a wine and alcohol bar. The red and gold furniture in the sitting areas made Kareema feel like she stepped into a medieval palace. The back wall of the room made an open closet filled with men's clothes on one side and women's clothes on the other. Kareema could see a large tub past the wide case opening that separated the two sides of the open closet.

She ran her hands over the women's clothes that were on hangers. "I know you don't think I am going to wear another broad's clothes."

"Those are brand new and all yours. The staff shopped for you after I binged all your social media

84

videos. If anything doesn't fit, let them know and they'll have it exchanged."

"Anyone ever tell you that you're a stalker?"

"No, but from you I will take that as a compliment."

Kareema stepped into the room on the other side of the closet walls. The bathroom was as large as Koraan's new room. She admired the large soaker tub that sat under a window. Kareema knew she would get used to long baths in it real quick. On either side of the window were separate vanities. Quickly eyeing the products that sat on both, she found which one was hers. It was full of designer perfumes and other cosmetics. The sound of the shower coming on caught her attention. When she turned, Octavius was shirtless.

Kareema couldn't take her eyes off his body. He was much more cut than what she thought. And tatted. The man had tattoos all over his chest, stomach, and arms. She watched him as he undid his belt and pants. He let them fall off his hips and stood there watching his instant girlfriend.

His imprint was impressive, and had Kareema licking her lips and wondering what it felt like to have that python between her lower lips. Intentionally slow, he pulled down his boxer briefs, paused to let her have a good look, then walked into the large shower.

She watched him as water from multiple spouts hit his body. The only thing that separated them was a tall glass wall and space. Both of which Octavius was about to correct.

"Kareema," he called to snap her out of the trance she was in. "Shower. Now."

She walked up to the glass and removed her clothing one item at a time while holding eye contact with Octavius. Whenever the glass wall steamed up and cut off their eye contact, Octavius wiped his hand across it.

Once she was naked, she went into the shower, then came to a sudden stop. "I need a shower cap. I just had the weave installed two days ago."

Octavius walked over to her. She thought he was about to get one for her, instead he grabbed her up by her waist with one arm and took her deeper into the shower.

"My hair!"

"Shut up. I can have someone here to install a new weave on your head every single day. So, if I want you in the shower with your weave on, that is what the fuck is going to happen. Do you understand me?"

"Octavius—"

"Are you mine or are you mine?"

"Don't you think we are—"

"Stop playing with me, Kareema. Stop acting like you didn't want to hop on this dick the moment you saw me in that office today. Quit acting like you don't want me to sink my dick deep into you right now and to do it every fucking night from here on out. Now, for the last time… are you mine or are you mine?"

"You scare me." The words came out rushed from Kareema's mouth. Octavius backed up to the opposite shower wall and waited for Kareema to explain. "I didn't mean to offend you."

"I'm waiting on you to explain so I can decide if I should be offended or not."

"Okay. I appreciate everything you are doing for me and my… Koraan. You must understand that this is a lot for a person to take in and wrap their mind around."

"What's so hard, Kareema? That I'm willing to do any and everything to protect you? Giving you and *our* son a better life, your mother too, and all I'm asking in return is that you give yourself to me and be mine?"

"I'm not a possession or piece of property, Octavius."

"I'm not trying to treat you as one. Would you have preferred if I whipped out my dick in the office for you to suck then and do nothing but pay off the first one or two people to sue you?"

Kareema didn't want to admit that was exactly what she had in her head when she came to his office. "Do you want to get to know me?"

"I've wanted that ever since we got off the phone yesterday. From the first video of yours I watched, I knew you were a woman that deserved everything, and I wanted to be the one to give it to you. For you to be by my side as queen of everything I've built while I help you flourish. This was never about sex. I could have a train of women here like that," he snapped his fingers, "if that was all I wanted. I want you, in every way, more than any female I've ever desired. Was I wrong about you wanting me?"

Kareema shook her head. "No… it's just—"

"Just what?"

"That is like the third time you've interrupted me since we've been in the shower."

He put his hands up.

"It's not you that scares me, to clarify. This has been like an avalanche that could bury me while it changes the landscape. I get that it's an avalanche for me either way and that is the part that scares me. There is no way for me to navigate this and guarantee I can still breathe, so forgive me for trying to hold my breath for a little longer."

Octavius nodded his head and thought over his words. "You may feel you are in an avalanche, but I am the boulder you stand against to keep from being swept away and buried so you can live another day."

Kareema had no response.

Octavius took slow steps towards her. "I am what ensures you don't have to hold your breath ever again. As long as you are faithful to me and our family, you never have to worry about if you will get to breathe again." He was standing so close to her she could feel his body heat. "Are you going to let me be your boulder and shelter you, or will you hold your breath until you pass out, guaranteeing you'll be buried alive because you can't possibly navigate while unconscious?"

Kareema nodded.

"Say it."

"I'm yours."

Chapter 7

"Say it again." Octavius demanded.

"I am yours."

Without warning, Octavius picked Kareema up and pressed her into the glass shower wall he watched her through a few minutes before. He kissed her hard and possessively. Once again, it overwhelmed her, but instead of fighting it, Kareema relaxed and gave into it. Octavius moved his arms under her thighs and pushed her up the wall until her pussy was directly in his face.

"Oh. My. God," Kareema moaned. She had spent the last two years focused on her son and getting her bag that it had been a while since Kareema had been intimate with anyone. Octavius had her toes curling. She held onto his head for balance and moved her hips, grinding into his face as he sucked on her clit. "Fuck!"

He moved his lips a little lower and stuck his tongue into her warm slit and moved it back and forth. Kareema rode his face just like that while he rubbed her clit with his fingers.

"Don't stop. Octavius, don't stop. Don't… aaahhh… fuuuuuuck."

Kareema's body shivered as she became silly putty in Octavius' hands and mouth. He maneuvered her body down his until her legs were once again around his waist.

"Look at me," he said.

She did.

"Keep your eyes on me."

Kareema nodded.

"Say it," he growled.

"I'll keep my eyes on you."

As soon as the words were out of her mouth, Octavius was plunging his dick deep into her. "Fuck, you are tight."

Kareema did all that she could to not close her eyes at the feel of him. He filled her up and stretched her walls like the couple of men from her past never did. Not that they weren't packing, but Octavius was hung like a horse and thick like an elephant. His strokes were long and powerful, and he knew how to fuck with all his dick.

"Say it again."

"What?" she asked.

"Say. It. Again." He said each word with a stroke.

"I'm yours. All yours."

Octavius stroked harder and Kareema's natural nails dug into his back, drawing blood that mixed with water and ran down his body. He didn't seem to mind the pain.

"Fuck, Octavius!" Her legs shook.

"Cum! Keep your eyes on me and cum on this dick."

Not that she had much of a choice, but Kareema did exactly as Octavius said with loud moans. She never kept her eyes on her partner while having an orgasm. It was the most intense thing she had ever felt before. Her entire body was limp, but Octavius was still going strong.

In Over Her Head

Needing him to slow down, she kissed him slowly, and he responded in kind. His strokes slowed to match their kiss. Unlike their other kisses, this one didn't make Kareema's feel like she was being suffocated. Their tongues danced together instead of Octavius' overpowering her.

She moaned as they kissed, and Octavius stroked harder. As he did, Kareema moaned louder. He reached up, put a hand around her throat, and pressed her against the shower wall while he took a step back. He stretched Kareema out with just her head, neck and the top of her shoulders touching the wall and her legs wrapped around Octavius' waist. With his other arm, he opened her up to him more by positioning her left leg over his right shoulder. With a firm grip on her small waist and the other hand around her neck, he fucked her mercilessly.

Kareema's titties bounced from the jarring thrusts. She'd never been manhandled in such a way, but she loved every second of it. Though his grip on her neck was firm, it wasn't too firm to restrict air. She always had a fantasy of being choked while fucked, but she never expressed it and her previous partners never took it upon themselves to do it. Before she knew it, another orgasm was on the verge of popping off.

Octavius grunted louder and louder with each intense stroke. He felt the clenching of Kareema's walls as she orgasmed, and it triggered his own. He emptied himself into her as they moaned swear words together.

He let her legs go and she slide down to the shower floor. Stepping back into the main showerhead, he looked down on the woman that was now his in every way that mattered to him. "This is how I will leave you every night. You will never need another man. Best believe, I'll slide into your pussy throughout the night. And you know why?"

Still panting from their excursion, Kareema answered between breaths. "Because... I... I am yours."

"Damn right."

In Over Her Head

Chapter 8

Several days had passed since that fateful day Kareema walked into Jones & Associates. She, Koraan, and her mother, Lilla, were living a completely different life than before. Anything they wanted was at their disposal. All they had to do was ask. Lilla and Mr. Knowles bumped heads about how the kitchen should run, but other than that, everything was all good. Koraan seemed to enjoy having a father around and Octavius doted on him so much that a stranger would not know the boy wasn't his blood. He even called in a favor to have the birth certificate amended to have him listed as the father without going through the court. Koraan went from being Koraan Michael Monroe to Koraan Octavius Jones with a simple phone call. Still, Kareema wanted more for and of herself.

In Over Her Head

The instant family sat at the dinner table having dinner. Kareema was fidgeting at the table.

"What's wrong?" Octavius asked.

"Nothing."

"Don't lie."

"I'm not."

"You're restless. You've been that way all week."

"I'm bored. I have nothing to do with my time."

"We can't start a business for you just yet. We've gone over this."

"It's not that. I have nothing to do. My mom keeps Koraan at her house most of the day. You leave to run your business every day. I can't even fix myself something to snack on without being scolded out of the kitchen. I'm the only person in this house with no purpose."

"Your purpose is—"

"Don't say be your queen."

Octavius put his fork down and wiped his mouth with a napkin. "What do you want to do, Kareema?"

"Anything!"

"Like what? Name it. If it doesn't risk exposing you, I will make it happen."

Kareema hadn't actually thought about what it was she wanted to do. She looked around the room and noticed the side of the suit standing guard just outside of the dining room. "Shoot."

"Shoot?"

"Yes. Learning to shoot will give me something to do, so I don't feel like I'm losing my mind. You showed me the gun range on the property. I wouldn't have to leave, and you can pick a Suit to teach me."

"A Suit?"

"All of your henchmen wear suits."

Octavius stared at her for a bit.

Kareema tried a different approach. She nodded to the chessboard that sat against the wall opposite Octavius. "A queen has to protect her castle, her heirs, and her king." She knew there was no way Octavius would argue with that, and he didn't.

The next morning, Octavius drove Kareema to the gun range in a golf cart. It was past where the cabins and stables were. When they walked in, a Suit was there waiting for them.

"Kareema, this is Charlie. Charlie, Kareema. He's going to give you lessons twice per week on handling a gun. Charlie is ex-marines and the best marksman I have."

Kareema and Charlie shook hands.

"Charlie," Octavius said.

"I'll teach her everything she needs to know."

Octavius gave Kareema a deep and passionate kiss. She had to catch her bearings when he pulled away from her. He patted her ass before departing to the house to leave for the day's business.

"What's first?" Kareema asked.

Charlie walked over to a table that had everything from handguns to rifles and shotguns laid out on it. "First, you are going to learn what each gun is and how to dismantle and assemble them. Once you can identify them and put them together, we will start practicing with targets."

It disappointed Kareema that she wasn't going to shoot any guns today. She was determined to be an excellent student and absorb all that Charlie was going to teach her. She didn't have anything else to do.

The two of them didn't talk about anything else but guns during her first session, but her second one, Kareema decided to do some probing. "How did you go from a top army marksman to working for Octavius?" Kareema asked while she slid the floor plate of a pistol's magazine clip into place and continued putting the gun back together.

"I joined the army right after high school. Did three tours in the Middle East until I got shot in my knee and needed a knee replacement. I was damaged goods, so they discharged me but didn't help me with anything in the real world. My grandmother ran into some trouble with her then landlord and Octavius stepped in and hired me in exchange when he learned about my background."

"Is that how he and his father got most of their staff? Individuals and families who were in trouble and had no option but to take what they offered?"

"So that is how he got you, Saucey."

"Saucey?"

"You." He points at me. "Saucey. Your sauce that got you in trouble."

Kareema's eyes got big with worry that all she had given up, all that Octavius had done to protect her, was now in vain.

"Don't worry. I'm not going to expose you. But I saw your videos before he deleted your account. There are still some duplicate videos out there. Knowing Octavius, they won't be available for much longer." They stared at each other for a moment.

"He's protecting me. More than anyone in my life ever has. I didn't ask him to do it," Kareema said to break the silence.

"He made you feel as though he was your last option, so he could be your savior. Ask anyone around here. He can't get anyone on his payroll without taking advantage of their situation. That way, they always feel indebted to him. Octavius isn't the king of anything but manipulation."

"His tactics are… nothing short of bullying, but his heart is in the right place."

"Hmph. Bullying with a good heart? That's a thing?"

Kareema put the last piece of the pistol in place. She didn't want to discuss Octavius any further.

"Let me give you a piece of advice, Saucey. Keep your guard up and keep your wits about you."

"What is that supposed to mean?"

"Don't get too attached to him. The slightest betrayal and Octavius will send you and your mother away to never be found again. He may even keep your son. Falling in love with him is dangerous. It will be the final lock on the trap he's built for you, and you will give him the key."

Kareema thought over his words for a few seconds. She wasn't used to depending completely on another person, let alone a man. A part of her still yearned for her own thing to do, and to make her own money. Octavius has set up the lushest of prisons for her. She knew she had to find a way to get her own, just in case. "Why are you telling me this?"

"No woman who's ever been involved with a Jones' man has survived the relationship. Octavius' mother, Mrs. Colson's sister... they could still be alive out there somewhere, but no one here will ever know. I don't want to see the same thing happen to you."

"I didn't know you Suits were so caring. Most of y'all are drier than cornmeal."

"Suits?"

"That's all y'all ever wear."

Charlie released a big laugh. "Alright, Saucey. We are going to be good."

Chapter 9

"Thank you," Kareema said, as she laid on top of Octavius in bed, thinking about all of this.

"For what?"

"Everything. I mean, before I called your office, you didn't know me from a can of paint, but you saved my life and changed it for the better for me, our son, and my mom."

"When a man knows what he wants, he goes after it and does everything in his power to keep it."

"Why me though?"

"Because you are as insane as I am."

Kareema laughed. "I'm being serious."

"I am, too. Only an insane person would add milk to a milk-based product with a bunch of other shit and pass it off as something edible."

"Hey!"

"That's what you did. I'm just saying I admire the drive and ambition, even if the innovation was a little off. But you somehow got hundreds of people to buy a product they should have known better than to buy. Imagine what you can do with a legit product. You can have a substantial business one day, if given the right tools."

Kareema ground into his groin. "Are you the right tool?"

Octavius gave her a deadly look. "Who else would be the right tool?"

"I was just joking, dang. Calm down."

"I don't joke about that."

"Got it." Kareema paused for a beat. "Is your father's old mistress why you take commitment so seriously?"

Octavius patted her ass to tell her to let him up. He got out of the bed and walked over to his side of the open closet. "Infidelity nearly killed me before I even knew what it was. It is something I won't stand for."

"What happened to your ex-girlfriends?"

"I don't have any ex-girlfriends."

This intrigued Kareema. "You mean this is your first relationship?"

He turned to her with some clothes in his hands. "I fucked… a lot. I tried to date, but none were willing to fully give themselves to me. That is, until I met you." With that, Octavius laid the clothes out on a chair and walked into the bathroom.

Kareema stayed in bed, thinking over his words. Sure, Octavius could be a lot, she thought, but he gave a lot in return. She counted herself as the lucky one.

When he finished with his shower, Octavius walked into the bedroom with only a towel around his waist. "I have to go out of town for business for a couple of days. My sister is moving back in today. She's been away at school."

"Sister? I didn't know you had a sister."

"Alana. She is your age. No, she's a year younger than you. You two should have fun, though."

"She's going to be here to babysit me?"

"Actually, I need you to babysit her. Yes, you two are the same age, but she is a bit of a wild child.

This is her home, too. Her room is just in a different wing. I have already instructed her she is not to take you off the grounds or post any pictures of you on her social media pages."

"Are you two close?"

"Not particularly. Besides the six-year age gap, she was my mother's joy, and I was my father's pride. I would run the family business, granted I changed said business, and she would… be spoiled."

"Didn't you say she was away at school? Sounds like she wants to make her own way in some form."

"Alana has changed majors and schools as many times as we've fucked."

"Oh."

By this point, Octavius was fully dressed in his classic black dress shirt, gold tie, and black dress pants. She watched him as he put on diamond studded cufflinks.

"You rarely wear those," she said.

"Not when I'm in the hood. I know I'm respected, but I'm not stupid. Folks will have no problem jacking me for my shit if they felt I was flashing it in front of them. When I have business elsewhere, I dress the part. When I have business in the hood, I simplify it."

Kareema watched him as he packed a bag, and she suddenly felt a pang at the thought of him not being there. He was such a large, overbearing figure that him not being there made everything feel too big. "I can't go with you?"

"Someone needs to be here with my sister."

"*Here* has an entire staff."

"Family. Alana needs family here. Plus, she is excited to meet you and Koraan. As crazy as she is, she will make a fun aunt, I think." Octavius noted the sadness in Kareema's face. "I'll be back in two days. We can spend two entire days in bed when I get back."

"I don't think my body can take that," Kareema says with a laugh. "You keep me sore as it is."

"So, you always know who you belong to."

Kareema put her arms up in the general direction of the room. "How could I ever forget!"

After getting dressed and getting her son off to her mom, Kareema went in search of Mrs. Knowles.

She found the older woman in the laundry room folding towels. "Here, let me help you," Kareema said.

"No need for that, ma'am. I've been doing this myself for decades. No need to change that now."

Kareema smiled. Mrs. Knowles always admonished her gently. "May I ask you something?"

"You may, but that doesn't mean I know the answer."

"What can you tell me about Octavius' sister?"

"Alana?"

Kareema nodded her head.

"You needn't worry about her. She's a good girl when she has something to focus on other than her brother."

"Were they close?"

"Mhm. Oil and water, those two. She always wanted their father to teach her the business and to trust her with some part of it, like he did her brother. He refused. She resented both of them for it. She didn't feel heard and respected, like Sir Octavius. So she would act out from time to time, which neither her father nor brother had the patience for. She needed a steady hand and constant love from her family after her mother left, and Alana never got it. Poor thing was off in boarding school when her father died. She begged her brother not to send her back, to let her finish her last year of high school here, and he did. I think he regretted doing it shortly after because she always tried to insert herself into business affairs. Sir was more than happy when she went away to college."

"Do you think she's still jealous of her brother?"

Jealousy is a stubborn beast. It doesn't go away easily. Alana's been away for a few years now. We will all know soon enough, I guess. I will say this, it's best if you don't try to get between them. If a problem arises, let them work it out on their own.

Kareema thought over Mrs. Knowles' words. She's been with this family a long time and has seen them at their best and worst. "Should I keep my distance from her?"

"Alana? No. That will only make her more determined to cause a problem with her brother, I'm afraid. Befriend her. You just may be the bridge to bring them closer."

In Over Her Head

"I don't want that responsibility."

"It's not your responsibility. We don't always have control over the roles or positions life puts us in. I meant no harm."

Chapter 10

Kareema stood in the foyer with Mr. and Mrs. Knowles, and Koraan, as they waited for Alana to come up the steps. She was taking her time, stopping to yell her greetings to various staff as she saw them on the grounds.

"Is she always that loud?" Kareema asked.

"That girl was born loud," Mrs. Knowles says with a laugh. "That is why I nicknamed her Horn."

Mr. Knowles joined his wife in laughing. "The loudest human I've ever seen, and I served in the Navy!"

Kareema had no clue how that compared, so she fake-laughed as if she knew.

When Alana finally made it through the enormous front doors, she immediately went to Mrs. Knowles and gave her a big hug. "Mrs. Knowles!"

Alana exclaimed while saying the woman's name slowly.

"Oh, my Horn. Let me look at you." The older woman held the younger out at arm's length. "You've always been such a pretty girl."

And Alana was more than pretty. She had the same light complexion and dark brown eyes as her brother, but with a wider nose and thicker lips. Alana was almost as tall as him, too. She stepped out of Mrs. Knowles's embrace while moving her waist length braids to one side.

"Mr. Knowles!" She embraced him. It wasn't as long as her embrace with his wife, but it was just as warm.

"I have a big bowl of your favorite salad in the fridge and plenty of pepper jack cheese to get you through the summer," he told her.

"You're the best, Mr. Knowles."

She turned her attention to Kareema. "Have you had his cucumber, tomato, and onion salad?"

I shook my head.

"Oh, girl, you must get some of this. He uses raspberry vinaigrette instead of vinegar and lemon juice. I can eat it all day. Now, let me check you out." She stood back, looking me up and down. "I always assumed my brother had women, but he never let me meet one. He has good taste, that's for sure." Alana licked her lips.

"Thanks. You are gorgeous, too. This is our son, Koraan," Kareema said.

"Oh, my god!" she screeched. "He is soooooo cute. Come here, man!" She took the boy from Kareema's arms. "I'm your auntie Alana."

Koraan put his hands over his ears, and it made everyone laugh, except Alana, who declared that we all go eat.

Alana wasn't lying. Mr. Knowles's salad was excellent, and she ate a god-awful amount of it.

"Besides your banging body, what made you so special that my brother will share everything with you?"

"According to him, I give him what no one else would."

"Meaning you haven't found his controlling ways a bit much then," Alana responds.

Kareema takes a moment to respond. "That's how he is. It's how he loves."

"He told you he loves you?" she asked, like the thought of him doing so was the craziest thing she ever heard.

This time, Kareema doesn't respond. Octavius had never said the words to her, but she figured he must have felt something for her with everything he's done for her and Koraan.

"Are you in love with him?"

"I could see myself loving him. Right now, this is just a big change."

"I've never, and I mean never, have heard my brother tell anyone he loves them," Alana stated. "I don't think I've ever heard him use the word, but he loves control. That's a trait he picked up from our father, I guess. Keep your heart for someone who wants it. Give everything else to Oct."

It shocked and confused Kareema that Alana would suggest she cheat on her brother. "I don't think your brother would take such a betrayal well."

"Who does? It's betrayal. You just have to be good enough to not get caught."

The way Alana stared at Kareema made her uncomfortable. She had to change the subject. "How long will you be home?"

"Oh, I don't know. I am thinking about taking a year off from school so I can figure out what I want to do, what interests me. I was going to travel during the year, but Oct has a girlfriend now and I must get to know her better," Alana said before reaching across the table to hold Kareema's hand in hers.

"It's time for Koraan's nap," Kareema said while abruptly standing up. She grabbed her son and headed upstairs as fast as she could.

Inside Koraan's bedroom, Kareema caught her breath. A woman had never flirted with her so openly before. Outside of the first time she went to his office, Octavius didn't flirt with her. Kareema had to admit that she enjoyed being flirted with.

She also had to admit that Alana was going to be a problem for her. Another problem in her life that she did not know how to get away from. She also wasn't sure if she wanted to.

In Over Her Head

Chapter 11

With Koraan down for a nap, Kareema entertained herself by the pool. Donned in a two-piece bathing suit, wide-frame sunglasses, and headphones, she listened to music while soaking up the sun.

Kareema never thought she could live such a charmed life. She laughed at the thought of it. All it took was a few people claiming they got food poisoning from her sauce. A sauce they and hundreds of thousand other people saw her put on food but never actually eat herself.

Her laughter was interrupted when she felt liquid dripping onto her stomach.

Kareema opened her eyes and took off the sunglasses. Alana was standing over her with a bottle in her hand, pouring its contents onto her. "Hey! What are you doing?"

"Relax. It didn't look like you had any sunscreen on." Alana dropped the bottle onto the ground and started rubbing it into Kareema's skin.

"We're Black. We don't need sunscreen."

"Says every Black woman who can't figure out how to get rid of the hyperpigmentation on their face."

"Hyper what?"

"Never mind. A Black woman made this just for Black people. Hold still." Alana rubbed the sunscreen onto Kareema's stomach in slow circles. Her hands creeped up Kareema's body little by little with each rotation. Kareema held her breath when Alana's fingertips brushed the underside of her breasts. Thinking Alana would go over her bikini top, she gasped in surprise when they didn't.

Alana looked into Kareema's eyes as she massaged her breasts. She loved the way Kareema whimpered under her touch. "Does my brother touch you like this?"

Kareema shook her head. It was the truth. Sure, Octavius fucked her well, but that was all he did. Fuck. He's eaten her pussy but had never touched her breasts other than while he was drilling into her. Maybe that was why she didn't stop Alana.

"Pretty ass," Alana said.

"Wait, cameras," Kareema said, remembering that Octavius told her there wasn't a part of the property that he couldn't see at any given time when he took her on a tour her first night there.

"I turned the ones on the pool deck off before I came out here. I told you, all you need to do is not get caught."

Kareema arched her back, pushing her breasts into Alana's hands.

"Pretty ass. I bet your pussy tastes good, too."

"Kareema LaShae Monroe!"

Kareema jumped up and saw her mother walking up from the other side of the pool. She quickly adjusted her bikini top to cover herself. "She's just rubbing sunscreen on me, momma."

"Since when do Black people have to wear sunscreen?"

"To keep from getting hyper..." Kareema looked to Alana for help.

"Hyperpigmentation. That's what the dark spots along your chin are called."

"The only thing about to get hyper is my blood pressure," Lilly said. "Do you want to explain to me why you are letting this thang rub on your breasts after this man has vowed to take care of everything for you?"

"This is Octavius' sister, Alana. Like I said, she was just rubbing sunscreen on me."

"Sister, you say?" Lilly questioned while looking Alana up and down.

Kareema nodded.

"Is this sister a lesbian?" Lilly asked.

"Momma!"

"I'm a lover of all beautiful things, ma'am. You have a beautiful daughter."

"Kareema, don't you mess up this good thing we all got. Do you have any idea of the stress you put me through when I checked my voicemail that day you took off?"

Kareema had to fight to keep from rolling her eyes as her mother went on about *her* stress again when she got a free upgrade.

"The police wouldn't take me seriously when I told them you were missing and played them the voicemail."

"They didn't take you seriously because Octavius had already informed them to ignore anything that came in about me. I've told you this multiple times."

"Men in black suits I had never seen before came knocking on my door in the middle of the night, saying they were taking me to you. I had to leave everything behind, including my cat."

"Omg," Kareema said under her breath, while Alana sat there soaking up the dramatics. The cat her mother referred to was the neighborhood cat that everyone fed and would beat up any other stray cats. The cat was for the streets.

"We've always been a no-pets family," Alana interjects. She was getting a kick out of riling the older woman up.

"What are you doing up here, momma?"

"I came to get my grandson for a few hours."

"Well, I put him down for a nap just over an hour ago. He should wake up soon."

"And you should stay away from her," Lilly said while pointing a finger at Alana before she stormed into the house.

"I'm going to go to my room. My mother forbade my father from putting cameras in my room since the security detail was all men. He took it a step further by removing the cameras in Octavius' then room, too. There may still be a set of separate cameras in your room, though." Alana paused after saying that, hoping that Kareema got her point. "You know where to find me if you want to visit."

With that, Alana left her by the pool. Kareema knew what Alana was telling her. She was going back and forth in her mind on if she should act on it or not. She had never been with a woman before and this woman was already being more attentive in ways Octavius hadn't thought to be.

Kareema was in the pool when her mother returned with Koraan in tow.

Lilly looked around for Alana. "Good. This is exactly what I wanted to see when I came back out here."

"You don't have to worry, momma. Alana was just messing with you because she saw it was easy to."

"Hmph. Don't you be easy and let her mess with you and everything you have going on."

"I won't."

"Alright. Well, I think I am going to have Koraan spend the night since I get so little time with him when his *daddy* is home."

"Okay. Have fun."

"You don't," her mother reminded. She walked off to the golf cart she left parked at the gate just beyond the pool.

Kareema knew what she told her mother was a lie. Alana intrigued her. She waited until she could no longer see the golf cart before going into the house.

In Over Her Head

Chapter 12

The door to Alana's room was ajar. She knew Kareema would not turn down the offer just as Octavius knew Kareema would not turn down his. The Jones siblings were very sure of themselves. Kareema knew she was playing with fire, but fire was so beautiful, intriguing, and warm. That is why moths could never stay away from it.

Kareema walked into the room and closed the door behind her. Alana had shut the curtains and candles were lit all around. The thought of Alana doing this for her made Kareema feel… desired. Alana walked out from her ensuite in nothing but a pair of high heels. Her long braids swayed with her hypnotic walk.

Alana caressed Kareema's face with the back of her knuckles. "I'm going to make you feel like a woman," Alana said.

The young women kissed. For Kareema, it was the perfect kiss. Hungry but gentle. Sensual, not rushed or dominating. Kareema wasn't sure of what to do with her hands, so she kept them by her side, while Alana's hands were on either side of her head. As they kissed, Alana's hands went down Kareema's neck and chest, then went under her arms and around to her back. They continued to kiss as Alana untied Kareema's bikini top and bottoms.

"Come with me," Alana whispered.

Alana led Kareema to the bed and gently pushed her onto it. She stepped out of her heels and brought Kareema's foot to her mouth. The sensation sent a jolt up her lover's spine that made Kareema's back arch. Alana kissed and sucked her way up Kareema's leg, stopping just at her apex. "Does my brother ever make you feel like that? Take his time with your body?"

"No."

"This is why women are so much better for women than men ever could be." Alana gave Kareema's clit a slow lick, then circled it with her tongue.

"Aaah."

Alana made herself comfortable at the end of the bed. She kissed, licked, sucked, and fingered Kareema's pussy until she orgasmed three times.

"Oh my God," Kareema moaned. She had never cum more than twice with Octavius and he most definitely never kept eating her past her first orgasm.

"You taste as good as I thought you would," Alana said as she laid kisses along Kareema's body while making her way up to Kareema's breasts. "I've been wanting these in my mouth since you let me touch them."

"Shit, you are so good at that," Kareema moaned as Alana suckled on her breasts.

"I'm good at so much more."

Alana hiked one of Kareema's legs up and adjusted herself until their clits were touching. Starting with slow strokes, she rubbed her clit against Kareema's. Kareema rotated her hips to match Alana's.

"Touch me," Alana said once they found their rhythm.

Kareema reached up and palmed one of Alana's titties.

"Yeah. Just like that." Alana threw her head back as she rocked her hips back and forth at a steady pace. They continued like this until exhaustion from multiple orgasms took over them.

Lying in bed with sweat glistening on their bodies, they cuddled each other. This was also something that Octavius didn't give Kareem after sex. He would lie on his back and have Kareema lie on top of him, but he never embraced her. He kept his arms folded under the back of his head.

"That was amazing," Kareema said.

"My brother never made you cum so many times, has he?"

"Never! I didn't think that was possible."

"This was your first time with a woman?"

Kareema nodded.

"Wait until I teach you some other positions and even strap you."

"Oh, you can't strap me. No, no, no."

"And why not?"

"Your brother will know. He fucks me every night to keep me sore, so I won't sleep with another man."

"Like a typical man, he only thinks about himself and other men. At the same time, I guess it is good I'm not another man then."

"Yes, but you are his sister. He is going to kill me if he finds out what we just did." Kareema started to get out the bed, but Alana pulled her back down.

"He won't. I made sure of it, unless you tell him. And it is not what we just did, but what we will continue to do."

"We can't do this again after he comes home."

"Does he still leave for work every day?"

Kareema nods.

"So, we will have plenty of opportunities to make each other cum again, and again, and again."

"You're going to get me killed. This is your brother's house."

"Half his. I own the other half. Our father left us both the property. Octavius alone got the business, most of the money, all the cars, the connections, and the respect. So, when I tell you we can keep fucking, that is exactly what we are going to do. Feed his ego and let him foot your new lifestyle. When he's not around, you're mine."

"Alana—"

Alana kissed Kareema to silence her objections. She kissed Kareema until she felt her body surrender before sliding two of her fingers inside Kareema's pussy.

Kareema shifted to lay her back on the bed to give Alana easier access. Alana took advantage of the position and suckled on Kareema's hardened nipples. She continued to bring Kareema to climax with her fingers.

Kareema was dizzy with ecstasy. She moaned and gripped the sheets as waves of pleasure rolled through her body. Kareema didn't know sex with anyone could feel like how Alana made her feel. She felt like she was floating as she got closer and closer to orgasm. Her body rocked and rolled with Alana's movements until it went stiff for a few seconds and then trembled from the orgasmic quakes.

"See, you're just as much mine as you are my brother's."

Those words snapped Kareema out of the pleasure bubble it had been in for the couple of hours she'd been in Alana's room. She jumped up out the bed, pushing Alana off her. Grabbing the pieces of her bikini, Kareema rushed out of the room, got dressed in the hallway, and made her way to the ensuite in her and Octavius' room. Stopping in front of her vanity, she stared at herself in the mirror.

"What the fuck!" Kareema only meant to befriend the girl, as Mrs. Knowles suggested she do. She didn't mean to open her legs to her. Kareema turned on the faucet and splashed water on her face. Returning her gaze to her reflection, Kareema gave herself an order. "You can't do that again."

In Over Her Head

Chapter 18

Kareema didn't stay away from Alana as she knew she should have while Octavius was gone. There was something about her that drew Kareema in despite the danger it posed for her and everyone she loved. Alana would turn the cameras off in whatever room she wanted to fuck Kareema in, then invite her to it. They had sex in the movie theater, pool, gym, and Alana's room several times.

Kareema wasn't sure how she was going to enjoy sex with Octavius again after his sister opened her eyes and legs.

The women were in the pool with Koraan having a good time. Alana splashed some water on the boy as his mother held him, which made him laugh and squeal with joy. Alana got closer to them while making suspense movie music sounds. Koraan laughed and kicked the water like he was trying to get away. When she got to them, she blew the boy raspberries on stomach then nipped at Kareema's nipple through her bathing suit and swatted her ass while the child was distracted with laughter.

"It's good to see my family getting along so well," Octavius says while standing by the lounge chairs.

"Octavius," Kareema exclaimed. "How was your trip?"

"Better than expected," he responded, before turning his attention to his sister. "Alana."

"Oct."

"If you don't mind, I'll catch up with my woman and son now. We'll see you at dinner."

"Go ahead."

"Kareema," Octavius said with a firm voice as he picked up two towels that were on the chair next to him.

Kareema got out of the pool as fast as she could. "Look, Koraan. Daddy's home!" She said the last part repeatedly as she made her way to Octavius. He took the boy and wrapped him in a towel while Kareema dried herself off and wrapped a towel around her body.

Octavius put a possessive arm around Kareema and took his family into the house. They ran into Mrs. Knowles as they made their way.

"Can you give Koraan a bath and get him dressed before dinner?"

"No problem, sir."

Octavius handed Koraan off to the housekeeper and went to his bedroom with Kareema. Once inside, he started barking orders.

"Take all of that off and get in the bed," he said as he began ripping his clothes off.

Kareema didn't hesitate. She was terrified that he saw what Alana did and knew they had been fooling around.

"Octavius," she mumbled as she tried to think of a way to defend herself.

"Two days," he growled. "I haven't been inside you in two days. That was far too long. You were right. I should've taken you with me."

Kareema stopped talking. There was nothing she could say. He got into the bed, hovered over her, spat on her pussy, then again on his dick. He plunged into her and growled.

"Just as I left it," he moaned.

She let out a sigh of relief. He wasn't mad at her. He didn't know. Octavius was just horny as hell. That allowed her to relax some, but memories of when Alana strapped her came to her mind. This was not remotely the same. Octavius fucked her for his pleasure. Alana fucked her for both of their pleasures.

"Yes, just as you left it. I'm yours. All yours." She said those words repeatedly to him as he fucked her.

When they were done, she laid on top of him and asked him about her trip.

"It was productive. My new investment should bring in a high return. I also scouted some placed for new strip malls."

"Doesn't America have enough of those?"

"Not enough that are in the hood and cater to it's needs. Every strip mall I put in place has a grocery store, eliminating the food desserts that plague so many inner-city communities. All the businesses in the strip malls must be majority Black-owned. I don't play that crap of other minorities establishing stores in our neighborhoods that cater to us, only to treat us like we're all crooks. They don't put any money back into the neighborhoods. That's not going to happen on my watch."

"That's good. Noble, even."

"You said that like though think I'm a monster."

"It's not that. You saved my life and have given me, my mother, and our son a new life. You gave Koraan a father. I may not understand you and your ways, but I could never see you as a monster. I mean, I still don't…" Her words got stuck in her throat.

"I still don't understand." Kareema stated.

"Understand what" he said as I laid on top of him with my head resting on his chest.

"Why me?"

"Kareema, it's been weeks now and you're still asking me that question. I already told you."

"No, you told me why you could make it easy for me to accept your offer. Not why I am the one you gave the offer to and why you would make such an offer. I mean, there are other ways to get a woman to be your girlfriend."

"My father raised me to be in control of the entirety of my environment and to be a ruler. He was the same way. Waiting for anything is not exactly a skill set I possess, which is why dating doesn't work for me. When I see something I want, there is no going back and forth or testing the waters to see if it works. When I watched your videos, I saw a beautiful woman who was in a unique enough of a position to give herself to me completely. A regular person would see that as taking advantage of your situation, but there is nothing regular about me. I see it as seizing an opportunity. You need to disappear and redirect your life. I can and am giving that to you. My kingdom needs a queen and heirs. You are giving that to me. It's a win-win situation for us both."

"Is love what you want? For us?"

"Love." He said the word like it felt foreign coming off his tongue. "I'm not the hearts and flowers type of guy. The examples of relationships I've seen taught me that hearts and flowers die. The things that keep any relationship going, loyalty, respect, honesty… I will give you in abundance. What I want at this very moment is to feel how your pussy grips my dick. That shit is unmatched."

I rotated my hips to grind my pussy on his tool that I could feel slowly waking up.

Lifting my chin, he kissed me deeply before pulling away. "I love the way you cum. You go silent and your eyes cross for a few seconds as your body stiffens before it shakes uncontrollably. I can feel that every day. I would feel it again right now, but we need to get ready for dinner."

With that, he swatted Kareema on the ass. She rolled off him and he went into the bathroom.

In Over Her Head

Chapter 14

Octavius, Kareema, and Koraan got to the dining table before Alana did. Kareema noticed the three place settings in the normal spots for the three of them, but there wasn't a fourth by them. Instead, the additional setting for Alana was at the other end of the table, directly opposite of Octavius' spot as the head.

Though she knew they weren't close, she feared Octavius knew more than what he let on to.

They were eating when Alana came down. "Thanks for waiting for me," she said as she took her seat.

"Those who aren't ready or forget their place get left behind," he responded.

It was in that moment that Kareema decided to keep her mouth shut for the duration of the dinner.

There was much more tension in their relationship than what she knew.

"And what place is that, brother?" Alana asked in a bitter tone. It was then she realized they had a deep sibling rivalry and why Alana always brought Octavius up when they had sex. Alana's attraction to Kareema was solely because she was Octavius' girlfriend. This realization made her feel used and, once again, dumb.

"See, I thought having you spend some time with *my* woman and *my* son would be good for you. Put you in the frame of mind to aspire to have a family of your own one day. Give you something to want to achieve. Instead—"

"Inspiration? For a family? This," Alana waved a hand at our end of the table, "isn't your *family*. That boy doesn't share your DNA. You bought this family... cheaply, I might add. Well, not so cheap considering all the shit you bought for them, plus the mother."

Alana's words stung and Kareema fought tears as she sat there, wishing she could disappear.

"Instead..." Octavius yelled, "I find you trying to get *too* close to what is mine, trying to replace me in MY FAMILY! Don't say you weren't because there hasn't been an issue with the cameras in years. Yet, you are here for two days and suddenly they are going on and off regularly, meanwhile you're on camera going in and out of the security room on a regular basis. You're not as smart as you think you are, little sister. I am the one who pays the staff and has their loyalty. This is why father left you nothing more than an allowance."

A pit grew in Kareema's stomach. For a moment she thought she and Alana wouldn't be found out, that she could have kept her affair a secret. She was a fool.

Octavius took a few deep breaths. "I have a proposition for you," he said in a calmer tone.

"And what would that be, Oct?"

"I want to buy you out your half of the property."

Alana laughed. "You can't afford to buy me out merely by collecting rents."

"The business is much larger and diverse than what you could have ever known. With that said, I can and will do just that." Octavius knocked on the table.

A suit came in with an envelope and placed it in front of Alana.

"Inside that envelope is the current value of the entire property. I took the liberty of writing out what half of that is on the paper since you've changed schools so often. I wasn't sure if you passed a math class."

"Fuck you, Octavius."

"You said my name, so I know you meant that." He smiled, laughing at his own joke. "The form behind that valuation is a check for one million above your half. I can tell you now that you won't get a better deal from me than that. I'm also fully aware that you've burned through most of your inheritance after I signed off on you having full access to it. This will replenish your account three times over what they were before. You will be a multi-millionaire again, should you accept."

Alana's eyes grew large while looking at the large check. That was the real reason she was home. She was almost out of money.

"Where do I sign?" she asked.

Octavius put a hand up. "This comes with conditions. You are never to step foot onto this property ever again. Should you ever have kids, they will have no claim to this property. You also are never to contact me or my family ever again. Whatever trouble you find yourself in from here on out, you're on your own. It is none of our business."

A tickle caught in Alana's throat. This time, Octavius' words and callousness hurt her. She cleared her throat. "You are just like father. He sent mother off with nothing more than a check and the clothes on her back when she got a side piece of her own. Served him right to die alone."

Kareema's head shot up. She didn't know this bit of information. Their father had mistresses, but the moment their mother had an affair, that was it.

"Is it a yes or no, Alana?" Octavius asked, ignoring what she said about their parents.

"What happens if I say no?"

"You will disappear with no access to the little funds you have left. After a year, I will have you legally declared dead and removed from the deed. If you want to talk about something being bought cheaply, option b is the cheapest for me. Care to take a guess at which one I'm more inclined to?"

Not that she was eating anyway, Kareema dropped her fork. She wanted to get out of there. She couldn't think of a way to protect herself while sitting in the middle of the madness. "I'm going to take Koraan up and read him a story."

"Stay," Octavius ordered. They stared at each other until Kareema nodded with tears streaking her face.

"Where do I sign?" Alana asked with a hoarse voice.

Octavius knocked on the table again. A different suit brings another envelope and places it in front of Alana with a pen. She opened it, pulled the forms out, and signed on every page that was flagged for her to do so.

"They will take you to a hotel of your choice that I will cover for one week. After that, you are on your own. Since you've been down here, my men have packed your things into a moving van and they'll put it into a storage unit. There are some bags with clothing and personal items waiting for you by the door."

Kareena wanted to look at Alana, but she didn't dare to. Instead, she kept her eyes on Koraan, who was across the table from her. She could see Alana wipe at her eyes before she stood and walked away.

It was eerily quiet in the dining room. Tears rain down Kareema's face like someone had turned a faucet on full blast.

"My mistake, I now realize, was telling you to never sleep with another man," Octavius stated.

"I'm so sorry. I wasn't thinking and—"

"We've long established that thinking past the initial thought is not your strong suit." He paused as his girlfriend sobbed. "If you ever…"

He let the quiet part of the sentence linger heavily in the air.

"I understand," Kareema cried.

Octavius knocked on the table again, and it made Kareema jump.

Once again, a suit entered with a manilla envelope, only this time they placed it in front of her.

"I know I had our son's birth certificate amended to have me listed as the father, but this document secures I will have full custody of him should you no longer be a part of this family for one reason or another. Sign it."

Kareema, with a shaky hand and much regret, signed it.

"The document behind it states the same for any future children we will have. Let's be clear, you will give me more. I have already disposed of your birth control pills."

Kareema stared at Octavius with angry tears streaking down her face.

"Sign it."

She did, though she didn't want to. Any fond feelings Kareema had for Octavius turned to hate. She didn't want more kids now, and he knew this.

"Go take a bath while I spend some time with our son."

Kareema looked back and forth from Octavius and Koraan. The last thing she wanted to do was leave her son with this madman, but what choice did she have? She had given herself over to him and just signed away her son and every child she will have with Octavius.

She regretted walking into his office that day.

In Over Her Head

Chapter 18

Four weeks later, Kareema was in the main bathroom pacing back and forth while Octavius sat on his vanity counter. He held his phone, watching the timer. Lying on Kareema's vanity was a pregnancy test. She was praying it was negative. The last thing she wanted was to be pregnant by him.

The alarm went off, signaling that enough time had passed. Kareema backed up against a wall. It scared her to look at it. Octavius hopped off his perch and went to the test. The smile his reflection showed told Kareema everything she needed to know, but wished wasn't true.

She was pregnant.

He went to her and put his hand over his lower stomach. "Be happy. We are building a family."

"What security do I have?" The words rushed out of her mouth.

"What?"

"If something were to happen to you. What… assurances do I have that they'll be taken care of and will inherit what is due to them as your kids?"

"You don't have to worry about that." He walked into the bedroom and Kareema followed closely on his heels.

"I'm their mother. Worrying about that is my job. How do I know that someone can't come in and kick us off the property if someone from the hood decides you are in the way of what they want to do?"

"No one is that stupid." Octavius began getting dressed for the day in his usual black dress shirt and gold tie.

"If you believed that, then you would wear your diamond cufflinks all the time."

Octavius paused and looked at her.

"You've secured their future for if something happens to me. They need to be secure if something were to happen to you. You can set up an administrator to handle everything if you are worried about me running off with the money or selling the property, which I wouldn't do, but still. If that makes you feel better about it, do it. Something just needs to be done."

"Where is this coming from?" he asked.

"Can you honestly say you haven't created enemies as the hood fixer? Like you said, we are building a family. I have nothing to leave our kids, but you have everything to leave them, just like your father did for you."

Octavius knew she had a point. He was more shocked that she knew what she was talking about and had put thought into it. "I'll set something up. I will also find you a doctor or midwife that can come here."

"Even for the birth?"

He nodded. "Hospitals are disgusting places. Plus, by the time this one is born, it would just barely be a year since you went phantom."

"Phantom?"

"Yeah. Like a ghost."

"I know what it is. It's just… is that my code name for your suits? I've heard them say that around me before."

"Yeah, that is your code name."

"What's yours?"

"God."

A part of Kareema wanted to laugh, but she chose not to. With the way Octavius controlled everything and everyone around him, she knew he took the name seriously.

"Have a good day," she said after he headed out of the room.

"You, too."

She knew he was going to see Koraan before heading out. Kareema convinced him to secure their kids' futures. She considered that a win in the battle ahead of her. Octavius did not know how correct he was when he said Kareema could be a great force if given the right tools. There's never a better tool or motivation for a woman than protecting her kids.

Chapter 16

As the months passed. Kareema realized Octavius was right. He didn't want her there just for sex. He wholeheartedly wanted a family, and she could give that to him instantly. However, because his parents' relationship was so fractured, he didn't know how to have a relationship with her. On the same hand, he was so great with Koraan and attentive to their baby, though it hadn't been born yet.

He was home at the same time every day. Didn't miss a meal with them. Afterwards, he would play with Koraan in his room, or take all of them out on a ride around the property. Koraan had to know the lay of the land that would one day be his, Octavius would say.

They had a tiff about who would tuck the boy in every night, as Octavius would dismiss her to do it himself. Kareema felt like he was trying to separate her from her own son. Similar to how she convinced him to file a will and trust for their kids, she got him to agree to let them do bedtime with Koraan together.

Octavius kept his word. He helped her find a passion that she could turn into a business. Kareema loved clothes, so she started an online boutique that would get a storefront a year after she had the baby. Octavius put an entire team around her, just as he said. She didn't have to do anything but shop for inventory. There was a person to put the pictures on the website, a team that came over once per week to package and ship orders.

There was one promise he did not keep, for which Kareema was grateful. He couldn't keep up with fucking her every night. His dick became sore from all the pounding he used it for. That cut down to every other day.

Kareema kept up on her shooting lessons with Charlie, only she started doing them every day since things went down with Alana. Charlie was an excellent teacher and Kareema became a solid shot with pistols, shotguns, and rifles. Shotguns were her favorite.

One day, she was at the range with Charlie when he asked her something that sent alarms off in Kareema's head.

"What are you planning, Saucey?"

She thought it best to continue to play as stupid as everyone thought she was. "Have this baby, open my store, maybe have a fashion show."

"Word on the streets is that an uprising against Octavius is building and there is a backer, a rich one. Of course, we told him this, but he doesn't seem to take it seriously. We haven't been able to prove it, but some of us think the rich backer is his brat sister. Though it could be some of his father's old dealers that will get out in a few months. They have every reason to have a vendetta against him, too."

This was all news to Kareema, but she wasn't surprised. "I never leave the house, Charlie. I wouldn't know anything about that."

"Yeah, I figured as much. That's not right, though, keeping you and your son here like prisoners."

"It's what Octavius thinks is best for us."

"What do you think is best for you?"

"If I knew the answer to that, I wouldn't have ever gotten myself in a place to be in this situation."

"Hmmm. Look, we've been doing this for months. I would think that by now we've established a solid friendship."

"I can't be friends with you. Octavius would have both of our heads."

"Fuck Octavius."

That wasn't the first time she heard Charlie talk about Octavius like that. "Why aren't you loyal to him like the rest of the suits?"

"He is a paycheck. A damn good one at that, but nothing more. So, are you going to keep it straight with me or not?"

"I told you, Charlie. All I'm trying to do is take care of my kids and my business. Nothing more."

"You didn't have friends before this? Other people besides your mom, who I will keep my opinions about to myself out of respect, that miss you? Anyone who would want to know where you are and how you are doing? You don't want to be free to come and go as you please? Saucey, what are you planning?"

"What do you want me to say, Charlie?" she yelled with her arms open. "Yes, I want all of that. Nothing but lawsuits face me out there."

"You would still have a life to live out there instead of being a baby making machine for 'the god'," Charlie said while doing air quotes around Octavius' code name.

"If I kill him, if I'm suspected of harming him, I lose my kids," she said, barely above a whisper.

It was silent while Kareema got her emotions under control.

"Like I said, there will be an uprising. You just need to be ready for when it happens. Trust me, you will know when it does." He stepped closer to her, picked up the clip to a handgun and loaded bullets into it so on camera it would look like they were still doing their lessons. "There is a gun safe hidden in a wall in damn near every room in the main house. Each of us *suits* have our own code that works on all the safes and there is a primary code that opens all the safes at once, no matter which one you put it into. Only Octavius has the primary code. My code is 10-32-16-60. Repeat it."

"Ten, thirty-two, sixteen, sixty."

"Again."

She repeated it as he passed her the gun. He pointed to the paper target on the other end of the range.

"Say each number as you empty the clip. I will tell you where a gun safe is in each of our sessions from here on out." Charlie stepped back and watched as Kareema committed the numbers to memory while firing the gun.

Kareema felt a little lighter knowing there was someone in her prison that was on her side.

Chapter 17

Kareema was on her knees, bent over the edge of the tub in the main bathroom with water that came to her hips. She'd been in labor nearly thirteen hours and she was exhausted, but the baby hadn't come yet. The midwife, Yolanda, rubbed her back while Octavius held her hand.

"I thought it was supposed to be easier after your first one," Kareema complained on winded breath.

"Most of the time, yes, but not always," Yolanda responded.

Another contraction came, and Kareema pushed and screamed. Screamed and pushed.

"Why is this so hard?" Kareema asked to no one.

"Aye," Octavius said. "You got this. Like you said, you did it before, you can do it again. Come on."

Her desire to kill him grew with every day, and this one was no exception.

"I need to adjust." She sat on one end of the tub with her back to it and her front facing the spouts. Octavius got in front of her. "Don't you think Yolanda needs to be there?"

He shook his head. "I want my hands to be the first he feels—the first to hold him."

"I'm right here, Kareema," Yolanda reassured. She was a slim woman with rich dark-skin and a kind smile. She positioned herself on the side of the tub. Yolanda did a check. "He is right there. On your next contraction, bear down as hard as you can."

The contraction wasn't far away. As soon as Kareema felt it, she took a deep breath and pushed.

"That's it," Yolanda cheered. "Push, push, push, push, push. Take a big breath and push again."

Kareema did and out came a healthy baby boy, right into Octavius' hands. He picked him up out of the water and cradled the squirming and crying baby in front of him.

"August Octavius Jones. I'm your daddy," he said to the child.

Kareema wished she had the energy and courage to kick him in his balls.

"Okay," Yolanda said, puzzled by the statement of the obvious. "Would you like to cut the cord?"

He nodded and cradled August in the crook of his arm and took the offered scissors with his free hand. Yolanda held the umbilical cord up and instructed him to cut between the two clamps. He did and gave her back the scissors while repeating to the baby that he was his father.

"Are you going to let me see him?"

He angled the baby so Kareema could see him.

"Octavius!" she exclaimed, with her arms out.

"She needs to nurse him. The sooner the better. We have to make sure he latches properly."

"He's my son. Of course, he's going to latch okay. More than okay."

Kareema rolled her eyes at his statement because he had paid no attention to her breasts in the time they had been together. Octavius passed her the child. He looked like a darker version of Octavius already. The old saying always was that your baby comes out looking like the person who irritated you the most during pregnancy.

"I'm going to tell Mr. and Mrs. Knowles, and your mom," Octavius said.

Kareema held her breath until she heard the bedroom door close.

"Is he always that… selfish?" Yolanda asked.

Kareema wasn't offended or embarrassed. "Yes."

"Is leaving an option for you?"

"I'm working on it," Kareema answered in a whisper.

Yolanda nodded. "Let me get him weighed, measured, and bundled. Then I'll help you get to bed. You did good. Very good."

Kareema opened the drain to let the water out and turn the faucet on so she could wash off. By the time she finished, Yolanda was back to help her out of the tub.

"I'm sorry about everything with him," Yolanda said after Kareema was settled. Kareema thought it was strange but she didn't question it.

"Thank you for everything."

Yolanda nodded and left.

Kareema rested in bed with her newborn sleeping in her arms. She and Octavius had made a beautiful baby. As the father expected, August took to nursing well. Kareema was relieved because the difficulty of nursing with Koraan made her feel like a failure as a new mom. It took a lot for her to get past that.

A couple hours later, Kareema heard hurried footsteps coming down the hall towards the bedroom. No one ever ran in the house. Charlie came bursting through the door with Koraan in his arms.

"Get up and get dressed. It is happening."

"What?" she said, confused.

"They rammed through the gate. A line of big trucks and cars with reinforced grill guards and guns. Lots of fucking guns. It must have been at least twenty of them."

Kareema was confused. "Twenty people came through the gate that has guards armed with machine guns?"

"Twenty cars! Or more. People are firing from all sides of the cars."

This got Kareema out the bed. She moved slowly and Charlie wished she could move faster, though he understood why she couldn't. Kareema slipped into some joggers, a tank top, and sneakers before going to Octavius' side of the open closet and hitting a button on the underside of a shelf. There was a click, then the shelving opened to reveal a hidden door. Kareema put in the code Charlie had her memorize.

The safe door opened to reveal an arsenal of firearms, loaded clips and magazines, and bullets. Kareema grabbed a loaded clip and put it in to a pistol before tucking the gun into the back of her sweatpants band. A few extra clips went into her pockets. She picked up an AR-15 style gun and a red light flashed overhead as she put a magazine into it. She turned and looked back at Charlie.

"Octavius entered the primary code to open all the gun safes. Come on, I have to get y'all to a safe room."

There were two safe rooms in the house: a small one behind the security room, and a much larger one in the finished basement. The smaller safe room was closer, but the path to get there was more open. They could get to the larger safe room via a narrow staircase in the wing they were in, but if Octavius' enemies caught them in it, they would have no way to escape.

"Any chance of getting to the garage?" Kareema asked.

"Let's figure that out after most of these fools kill each other," Charlie responded.

In Over Her Head

Chapter 18

Kareema, Charlie, and the kids made their way to the safe room by the security room, with Charlie carrying Koraan in one arm and August in a car seat in the other hand. Kareema led the way with the machine gun at the ready.

With her heart racing, Kareema took deep, steadying breaths as they moved cautiously through the house. She didn't think she would be so nervous about shooting someone after all the target practice she had. Most of the time, she imagined the targets were Octavius.

She slowed down when she heard voices in heated discussion on the landing of the grand staircase. The male voice was Octavius. The female voice was a familiar one Kareema hadn't heard in a while. She peeped around the corner to make sure it was who she thought it was. There stood Octavius and his sister, Alana, pointing pistols at each other.

"You thought you were going to take everything from me and give it to that whore and her poonanie turds?"

"We both know you aren't going to shoot me," Octavius says.

Pop.

A gun went off. Octavius grunted and stumbled back, but didn't go down. Alana shot him in the leg.

"Sure about that, Oct?"

"I gave you tens of millions of dollars! What more do you want?"

"I want everything father left you. Everything you were going to leave those kids, solely to keep me from getting it."

"You weren't getting it even if I didn't have kids."

"Take me to your new bundle of joy, it's brother, and their whore mother, so we can see how true that is."

Kareema revealed herself, coming around the corner with her gun pointed at Alana. "You aren't going anywhere near my kids."

"How do you even know she had the baby, let alone was pregnant?" Octavius asked.

"The midwife is the half-sister of a dealer you gave up to the police," Alana answered.

Out of the corner of her eye, Kareema watched Charlie put her kids on the floor and instruct Koraan to stay there. He got his gun out from under his suit jacket but stayed hidden behind the wall.

Alana smirked. "Did you think you were going to scare someone with that big gun?"

"Go to the kids, Kareema, and hide. I'll come get you when this is over," Octavius said.

"I have people watching both safe rooms. She was never going to make it there," Alana stated.

"Even father didn't mess with kids," Octavius said, trying to reason with his sister. "You really think you have it in you to harm two little kids? Koraan and August are your family, no matter how much you hate me."

Hearing his daddy say his name, Koraan took off towards Octavius' voice. "Daddy!"

The boy slipped past Charlie, who came out of hiding when he reached for Koraan. Out of reflex of seeing someone going towards Koraan, Octavius turned his gun from his sister to Charlie and fired twice without seeing who it was.

Charlie went down as deep red stains grew on his shirt. Alana took advantage of her brother being distracted and fired off her gun. She got two shots off, both landing on Octavius' side before Kareema responded with shots of her own, putting bullets into her former lover. Alana fired a third time as she went down, but the bullet went into the wall right above Octavius' head.

With caution, Kareema walked up to Alana's body as it laid on the wood floor. Alana struggled to say something as blood filled and spilled out of her mouth. Kareema kept the gun on her until her body stilled.

Once Alana was no longer a threat, Kareema turned her attention to Koraan. He was in the arms of the only father he'd known as Octavius was sitting on the floor, slumped against the wall. There was too much blood. She knew he would not make it. Kareema took August out of his car seat and took him to where his father and brother were. She helped Octavius hold the baby, as he was too weak to do it on his own.

"You're going to forget about me, but I will always watch over you, both of you," he said before pain caught in his throat.

"Octavius…" Kareema didn't know what to say. For months, she imagined killing him and now that he was dying, she wasn't as happy about it as she thought she would've been.

"I did the best I knew how by you," he said. "You needed more, but I did my best."

"I know," she whispered. Her heart was breaking for her boys, who were about to be fatherless and for herself. She was going to have to face a world where she was once again making decisions since Octavius would not be around to take care of everything on her behalf.

"It's all yours now. I left the bulk of it to you, Kareema. Don't lose it all by making more dressings, or any food, for that matter."

In Over Her Head

Kareema chuckled through the sob she had been holding in. "We'll be good, Octavius."

"Don't let them call no other dude daddy."

"I won't."

"I'm their… I'm…"

Octavius' head dropped, and he was gone.

Epilogue

Even in death, Octavius was still protecting Kareema. He set it up for Kareema to get a new identity if he murdered. Her new name was Queen Octavia Jones.

She rejected the name when she saw it on the I.D. & passport when his attorney gave her the papers for her new identity and fortune, but the name was so Octavius. It showed her he cared for her as more than just a bedmate and the mother of his kids. He wanted her to carry his name and for Kareema, now Queen, to see herself as a queen.

After the gunfight that claimed several lives, including her mother's, Queen moved to Laurel, Mississippi. However, she still owned the Jones family property where August was born. Laurel was a small town full of life and no one who knew her from her sauce mishap. She bought a house that was just enough for her, Koraan, and August, and two dogs. She was determined to raise her boys with a sense of normalcy. That was what Octavius and Alana didn't have in their lifetimes, and it cost them dearly.

They were going to know that their mother worked hard. That's why the opening of her brick-and-mortar boutique was so special to her.

She had her boys front and center with her as she cut the ribbon and posed for the local newspaper.

"Congratulations, Queen," visitor after visitor told her.

The grand opening was a success.

When she was back home, after putting the boys down, she went out to her small backyard garden she used as a memorial for her mother, Charlie, and Octavius. Kneeling in front of the stone marker for Octavius, she felt grateful.

"Thank you, Octavius. We didn't have the easiest time. I wanted to kill you myself, but I wouldn't be where I am now if it weren't for you. The boys are happy and healthy. I tell them how much you loved them every single day. I've met someone. Don't worry. I checked this time, and he is a lawyer. He is as legit as you wished to be, but with a more normal upbringing.

"He hasn't met the boys yet. I'm going to give it more time before that and I promise, if he sticks around, the boys will not call him daddy. Maybe some other variation, though."

She laughed, thinking about how much Octavius would object to that until bird poop landed on her shoulder. Queen shrieked and stood up. "Fine! No variation! You don't need to be an asshole about it."

A squirrel chirped, and she imagined it was Charlie laughing at her.

"Ha ha, Charlie," she said with a smile.

Before leaving, she looked at her mother's stone and apologized. Though Queen was grateful for her new life, she felt guilty that it put her mother in harm's way. She wasn't sure if she could ever forgive herself for that.

Despite the guilt she lived with, life was good. She no longer felt she was in over her head. No avalanche was threatening to take her out. She could breathe on her own and that air was so precious to her.

The End.

In Over Her Head

Porsha Deun

Acknowledgements

I am so very grateful for this story. It's the one that got me back into writing after taking a long, yet much needed break. By the time this one hits the market, it will have been over a year since I published a book. Thank you, Kareema, for choosing me to write your story.

There are a couple of people I want to thank. First, Audra Russell, thank you for your encouragement and the good laughs. You are truly one of my favorite people in the book community. Thank you for all you do for Black authors. I can't wait to get your reaction to this one!

Susan Andersen, thank you. I believe in divine intervention. I was trying to figure out my game plan to promote my books again when you said, "I'm good at social media marketing and you need to be famous." Ha! Thank you for your help with my social media and for believing in me before even reading one of my books.

Porsha Deun

A Note from the Author:

Thank you for reading my book! I feel honored, truly. Did you enjoy In Over Her Head? Be sure to leave a review on Amazon, Goodreads, Bookbub, or my Facebook Page!

You can preview and purchase the rest of my books on my website, as well as with your favorite online book retailer! Be sure to sign up for my mailing list while you are on my website. My Love Bugs get cover reveals at least a month before the public, as well as surprises and giveaways. www.porshadeun.com.

Love Lost Series
Love Lost
Love Lost Forever
Love Lost Revenge

Addict Series
Addict—A Fatal Attraction Story
Addict 2.0—Andre's Story
Addict 3.0—DeAngelo's Story
Addict 4.0—DeMario's Story

In Over Her Head

Standalones
Intoxic
In Over Her Head

Collections
Eyes of the BeholdHer

Children's Book
Princesses Can Do Anything!

Milton Keynes UK
Ingram Content Group UK Ltd.
UKHW010635040324
438885UK00001B/44

9 798990 151802